**Presented to
Mount Tamalpais
School Library
in honor of**

*Michele Caitlin Freed*

by

*Kate*

# THE
# Clay Ladies

## MICHAEL BEDARD
## ILLUSTRATED BY LES TAIT

TUNDRA BOOKS

Published in Canada by Tundra Books, *McClelland & Stewart Young Readers,*
481 University Avenue, Toronto, Ontario M5G 2E9

Published in the United States by Tundra Books of Northern New York,
P.O. Box 1030, Plattsburgh, New York 12901

Library of Congress Catalog Number: 98-61336

Canadian Cataloguing in Publication Data

Bedard, Michael, 1949-
    The clay ladies

ISBN 0-88776-385-5

1. Loring, Frances, 1887-1968 – Juvenile fiction. 2. Wyle, Florence, 1881-1968 – Juvenile fiction.
I.Tait, Les, 1949-    . II. Title.

PS8553.E298C52 1999        jC813'.54        C98-930679-8
PZ7.B381798C1 1999

We acknowledge the support of the Canada Council for the Arts and the Ontario Arts Council
for our publishing program.

We acknowledge the financial support of the Government of Canada through the Book
Publishing Industry Development Program for our publishing activities.

Design by Sari Ginsberg

Printed and bound in Spain
D.L. TO: 1660-1998
1 2 3 4 5 6                        04  03  02  01  00  99

Now that I am nearly big, I sometimes spend the weekend at Grandmother's house. I sleep in the big soft bed at the head of the stairs and listen to her move about below. When I am feeling brave, I creep across the cold floor to the window. The yard is wild and full of shadows, and at the window of the wooden shed back there I sometimes catch a glimpse of ghosts.

In the morning we eat porridge cooled with cream, and marmalade on toast, off plates the color of rose petals. We sit in the dim front room and play records, or take books down from the dusty shelves to read.

The shelves are lined with figurines. A plaster cat lies curled in sleep; two stately herons hold up books between them; a plaster frog waits patiently for plaster flies; a seated woman supports her child between her knees; an old man stares off into space and seems to listen while we read.

And on the top shelf, resting side by side, two plaster women sit and watch us all. Grandmother calls them the Clay Ladies. And this is the story she tells:

Back when I was a girl, on the street where we lived, there stood a house unlike all the rest. It was made of wood, painted red, with pointed windows and a steep, pitched roof. Pigeons roosted under the eaves. We called it the Church, for it had been once, though it was no more.

The house had been there long before the others on the street. Long before the sidewalks and the roads, it sat there in the midst of wilderness. Now, only its own little wilderness remained, an island in the midst of ordered things.

The neighbors complained. The grounds were a disgrace, they said. The paint was flaking from the house. Pigeon droppings soiled their roofs. Stray cats roamed at will about the place.

It was here the Clay Ladies lived.

hen I was very young, I would hide in the hedge in front of our house just to watch them go by. Down the street they would walk, talking all the while. They moved like majesty. One was tall and stout, the other small.

I watched them with a kind of awe. They were not at all like women I had known. They wore baggy trousers and men's stiff shoes, and one had her hair clipped short. With their berets pulled down over one ear and their regal way, they were like rumors of a strange new world to my small eyes.

I would peer through the webwork of branches as they went by, and look close to see if they were really made of clay.

They weren't, of course. They were sculptors. They made things out of clay. And though the neighbors thought them strange, the children often visited the Church to see the giant that stood guard inside the door, or to bring their sick or injured pets, for the Ladies had a way with wounded things. And when they left, the children often came away with a lump of clay. It was they who had given them the name.

I remember the first time I went to see them as if it were yesterday. It was spring, and I was playing in the yard. The magnolia was in bloom, the ground about it strewn with pale pink petals.

A cat was sitting on the grass beneath the tree. Completely still, a statue of a cat. It studied me with wide, unblinking eyes as I approached.

Then, from a place that seemed far off yet somehow near, I heard a sound. A frightened, muffled peep. The cat's paws parted, and a flash of dull brown feathers fluttered free and landed on the lawn between us.

The cat, unmoving still, looked up at me, then down at it. With one swift pounce it hid the bird beneath its paws again, as if it had never been. And again that frightened, feeble peep.

For a moment I was made of stone, not knowing what to do. Then I stamped my foot, clapped my hands. "Shoo," I shouted, and the cat fled to the safety of the bushes. It crouched there set to spring, its eyes fixed on the bird.

The bird sat on the grass among the fallen blooms. At first it did not move, but when I came close it fluttered a few feet through the air, then fell back to the grass again. It couldn't fly. I knew I couldn't leave it there, so I caught the bird and cupped it in my hands – a frightened, feathered thing. I knew where I should take it.

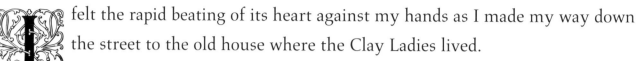**I** felt the rapid beating of its heart against my hands as I made my way down the street to the old house where the Clay Ladies lived.

A stray cat watched from atop the woodpile as I went up their walk. Pigeons took to the air with a startled snap of wings. I knocked on the door. First, silence; then a muffled shuffling of feet. The door opened and the tall one stood there, towering over me.

ello," she said. "What can I do for you, young lady?" I'm not sure I said anything. I showed her the bird and she showed me in. She told me her name was Miss Loring.

We entered through a shed, a shadowed place, stacked with broken things: boxes, broken stands, discarded casts, like junk washed onto shore from the sea. Then through another door and into the Church itself.

I don't think anything has ever struck me quite so much as that first sight.

he ceiling leapt up into light. The room was large and full to overflowing. Boxes stacked upon the floor; books and papers piled about upon the tattered furnishings; the floor blanketed with white dust and dropsheets.

But in the midst of all this clutter, sculptures everywhere. A sea of them – the larger standing free, the smaller scattered randomly on shelves and tabletops. Busts and figurines: a dancing boy beside a pot of daffodils; an Eskimo mother with her child on her back; a sea nymph flanked by sea horses colored green. And just inside the door, a giant goalie seven feet tall, standing guard on mystery. All so real, so silent, so still; as though they lay beneath some magic spell.

Uncompleted pieces stood about like ghosts, shrouded in damp sheets. A massive figure made of clay peered from behind a makeshift scaffolding.

**A**nd in the midst of this they lived. A huge fireplace stood against one wall, and before it a kind of clearing: a sagging couch; a clutch of chairs; a few old lamps, their cords strung like web strands through the air; a low table set for tea. The smaller woman sat there calmly carving a small block of wood. A cat lay curled among the shavings at her feet.

"Florence," said the first. "This young lady has something you should see."

She laid her work down on the table and looked up at me over her glasses – a small, sharp woman in a blue smock smeared with clay.

"What have you got there?" she asked. "A bird, is it? Let me see."

"The cat got it," I said. "I chased it away."

"Can't blame the cat," she said. "It's their nature to like winged things."

I watched the way she cradled the bird in her hands as she took it from me. Her hands were strong yet tender, in love with living things.

"It's a fledgling robin," she said. "It can't fly yet. It must have fallen from its nest." As she stroked its head, it peeped plaintively.

"Is it going to die?" I asked.

"It looks pretty lively to me. Why don't you leave it here with me a bit? There's an old cage around somewhere, I think. In a week or so its feathers will all be in. Meanwhile, you can come and visit it whenever you'd like."

went back every day. Soon the sense of strangeness dimmed; I no longer saw the flaking paint, the shadowed shed, the clutter everywhere. More than the bird, though, it was wonder that drew me there.

Florence had put the bird in a cage and hung the cage from a beam, well beyond the reach of cats. For there were cats everywhere, more cats than I had ever seen. They wandered in and out the open windows at will, prowled on silent feet like tigers in a forest. They curled up on chairs, on top of shelves, slept at ease among the statues. Then woke and stretched like sculpted cats waking.

And all these figures with them seemed poised upon the brink of waking, their stillness only sleep. As if beneath the stone, hearts beat. How strange it was to think that each one took its shape from formless clay.

The first day I returned, Florence reached into a large tub full of water near the door and brought out a lump of clay. She broke the piece in two and handed half to me.

On the far side of the room, Miss Loring stood upon the scaffolding – a board laid between two ladders. The wood strained dangerously beneath her weight while she worked calmly on the figure of a woman holding a baby.

"Don't worry," said Florence. "If she falls, she'll bounce. Never happy working on something unless she has to climb up to get to it."

Miss Loring laughed; the laughter sifted down like dust in the still air.

lorence motioned me to a chair near her worktable. She began to break off pieces of her clay, kneading it, molding it into a rough shape. She talked as she worked. From time to time she stopped and looked at me.

She introduced each cat as it came in. "The black-and-white is Peter. The tabby there is Michael. That's Marmalade. Once she was sick and wouldn't come down from the ladder, and we had to call the doctor, who had to climb up there to tend her. The black Persian there is Beautiful. Once, a visitor opened a drawer and found her sound asleep inside it. Almost had a heart attack, poor thing."

I remember still the feeling of the clay in my hand – cold and damp and slick. I pressed my fingers into it.

"Once you get the feel of the clay in your hands," Miss Loring said, "there's nothing else you want to do."

When I came the next day I found our pieces of clay wrapped in plastic, draped with a damp cloth so they wouldn't dry. Florence uncovered them and began to work. She took dabs of clay, applied them to the rough figure, then smoothed them flat with her fingers the way she stroked her cats. And soon I knew the figure forming there was me.

I sat in my chair and watched and shaped my little bit of clay. It was this, then that, then this again. A thing still forming.

I tried to move my hands in tune with hers. "It's like music," she said. "One shape singing with the next in harmony. That's not a thing that you can teach. You have to feel it, that's all.

"Try to feel the life in it. If it's not there, start again. Again and again and again. Keep at it till you can feel the life in the thing. Then, it almost makes itself. It opens from the inside, like a flower opening."

A fly was buzzing against the window, bumping, bumping, trying to get out. Florence put her work aside and went over to it. She caught it in her hand. "There, little friend," she said. "Is this what you want?" And she opened the door and let it out.

A week flowed by. Now, while we worked, the bird sat in the cage beside us. Its feathers had come in. Sometimes it sang, and all the cats would stop and listen.

"Nobody sees things anymore," said Florence. "A bird's legs don't go straight down from its body. See, they bend. You have to stop and take the time to look at things."

The piece was almost finished now. She smoothed and molded the clay with a wooden stick, cutting in the fine detail – a small clay child, holding something in her hands – as I sat holding the clay.

"There," she said finally. "It's done."

Miss Loring lumbered down from the ladder to look. "It's lovely, Florence," she said. "And what have you got there?" she said to me. I showed her the small clay bird that I had made.

he next time I came I found Florence back at work on her carving – a woman's form emerging from the wood. The bird was singing in its cage, a cat curled nearby, listening.

"Well," she said, "I think it's time we set our small friend free."

She took up the cage and went to the back door. The cat followed us out into the wilderness of yard. Tall oaks and slender ash trees, tangled shrubbery; wildflowers blooming by the long grass in the sun; a piece of sculpture, greened with moss, set among the trees, as if it too had sprung up from the ground.

We stood in a little clearing full of sun. She opened the cage door and reached in. "There, there," she said. "No need to be afraid, little friend." She held the bird in her hand and stroked its head. For a moment it stood still. Then it spread its wings and sailed into the branches of a tree.

"There," she said. "Now it's where it needs to be."

e walked back to the house. Miss Loring was up the ladder again, working on the sculpture of the mother and child. The clay figure sat on the table – a part of me there now.

I said good-bye, took my little bird of clay, and made my way slowly down the street. The sun was shining and I was looking, looking at everything.

The Clay Ladies are gone now. They died some years back. But a part of them is here still in the many things they made. They taught me more than I can say, and I'm glad to have them here watching over me.

**W**ell, it's time I got to work," Grandmother says.

 We go into the kitchen, and she takes her smock down from a peg and puts it on. It is a blue smock, smeared with clay.

We go out the back door and start down the little path that snakes through the wild grass to the shed. Through the window I can see the sculpted figures on the sill, behind them larger shapes shrouded in sheets like ghosts.

We walk slowly. For there are wildflowers blooming in the long grass. Buttercups and daisies by the score. We stoop to see, to feel the waxen stems, the tight buds shingled green, the flowers opening. A bee is buzzing in the chickory; a robin sings high in the branches of a tree.

And Grandma and I on the path, stopping all the way to look at things.

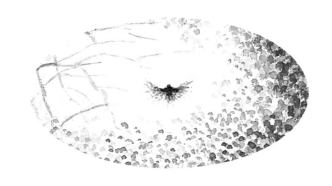